HERMAN AND THE ICE WITCH

by

Sarah Brown Weitzman

PURE HEART PRESS
MAIN STREET RAG PUBLISHING COMPANY
CHARLOTTE, NORTH CAROLINA

Acknowledgements:

The author wishes to thank the **National Endowment for the Arts** as the first draft of this story was written during the period of its support.

Library of Congress Control Number: 2011915224

ISBN: 978-1-59948-328-3

Produced in the United States of America

Pure Heart Press
Main Street Rag Publishing Company
PO Box 690100
Charlotte, NC 28227
www.MainStreetRag.com

*Dedicated to the memory
of my parents*

*Mildred Toole Brown
and
Philip E. Brown, Jr.*

HERMAN AND THE ICE WITCH

1

Anyone who has seen Bleak Mountain when a winter fog twists and curls around its peak can understand how the legend started. The fog rising over the distant mountain looks like whorls of smoke pouring from a great chimney. *The witch's chimney,* many said. They shuddered when they said it.

Of course, there are always those who will not believe anything they cannot prove. They scoffed at the notion that an evil witch lives on Bleak Mountain. Yet, had any grownup thought to ask him, Herman Lutt could have proven that the witch was real. She had written to him!

It was precisely because of this letter from the Baroness Meen as the witch called herself that Herman packed his few belongings into a suitcase and was now headed straight for her castle at the top of Bleak Mountain.

It was a difficult journey for a boy not quite twelve, especially in winter. All morning he was able to keep the mountain in sight as he made his way through the deep snow. By afternoon he came to a dark forest.

Here, the trees grew very close together. Overhead their branches, heavy with snow, formed a canopy so he no longer had a view of the mountain to guide him. Soon he began to worry that he might not be headed in the right direction. His suitcase seemed to be getting heavier. He almost doubted his resolve when he thought of the other boys in the orphanage who about now would be finishing a hot lunch and choosing sides for a fierce game of stickball in the yard. But just then, he was very pleased to see a field mouse ahead, struggling over the drifted snow.

"Hold on a moment," Herman called to the mouse. "Can you tell me the way to Bleak Mountain?"

"*Yow!*" shrieked the mouse with fright. He did a backflip in the air.

"Please don't run away," cried Herman.

But there was no possibility of the mouse running away as he had landed upside down in a soft mound of snow and was kicking and thrashing violently in an effort to get out.

Herman squatted down beside the now half-buried mouse. "Please don't do that," he called down the hole the mouse was deepening by his struggles. "I didn't mean to frighten you."

"The Baroness sent you!" the mouse sputtered in spite of a mouthful of snow.

"Not exactly," explained Herman, astonished that the mouse had mentioned the Baroness. All he could see of the struggling mouse was a tail and two spindly hind legs sticking up out of the snow. "I don't know how you could possibly have known that I have a letter from her."

"I knew it! I knew it!" wailed the mouse, his legs scissoring frantically through the air. "I'm done for."

"I can't imagine what's upsetting you," said Herman, quite at a loss to understand why the mouse was so frightened. "It's really difficult holding a conversation with someone who's upside down. I can barely make out what you're saying."

"Oh, dear. Oh, dear. She sent you. I'm done for."

"I'm trying to explain. The Baroness didn't send for me but I've come anyway." Herman bent over the buried mouse. "In fact, she didn't really invite me at all so naturally there weren't any directions in her letter. Now I think I might be lost."

The mouse was so surprised that he stopped thrashing about. "You *want* to visit her?"

"I'll bet you'd like to come up out of there. You can't be very comfortable upside down in that snow."

There was a silence.

"I'm not," the mouse said finally but rather huffily.

Herman took the mouse by tail and pulled him out of the snow like a cork from a bottle. "That's much better, isn't it? I certainly didn't mean to scare you, you know."

"Oh, I wasn't one bit afraid of you. I slipped and fell into this snow drift and then I couldn't get out."

"Of course," said Herman agreeing politely. "Let me introduce myself. I'm Herman Lutt."

"I'm Wallace," offered the mouse, still eyeing Herman suspiciously.

"I hope you can direct me to Bleak Mountain."

"SHE'S-A-WITCH!" the mouse exploded all in one breath.

Herman smiled broadly. "Exactly! Now we're getting somewhere. Exactly why I want to find her."

"Didn't you hear me? I said she's a witch, a WITCH!" The cords in Wallace's neck worked up and down. He started to back away from Herman.

Herman took the mouse by the tail. "Wait a minute. You needn't shout. I know the Baroness is a witch. That's exactly why I'm trying to locate her. I thought you were beginning to understand that. Perhaps you should read the letter she sent me."

"Then she *did* send you!" Wallace tugged at his tail frantically. "LET GO!"

"This is very frustrating. Every time I think I am making myself clear, you start shouting again and try to run away." He drew Wallace closer. "Her letter will explain everything." He took a crumpled envelope from his suitcase.

In spite of his fear the mouse was curious. "Is it really a letter from the Baroness?"

"Yes," said Herman proudly. "The first time I touched it I knew it was different from any letter I'd ever seen before." He juggled the letter awkwardly from hand to hand as he spread it out on the snow. "Feel it," he urged. "You'll notice at once how cold your fingers get."

Wallace squinted at the letter but he declined to touch it.

"The second thing you'll notice," continued Herman, "is the lettering. If you look closely, you'll see that the silver ink isn't ink at all. It seems to be ice!"

"The Ice Witch," groaned Wallace.

"Yes, she'd certainly have to be a witch to write in ice. Quite original but a little hard to read."

Wallace read:

Dear Herman Lutt:

The meeting you propose as a means of our exchanging ideas and staying au courant in the constantly changing field of witchcraft is very interesting. However, I cannot at this time extend any invitation to you of any sort, whatsoever. In short, do not come to Bleak Mountain.

Furthermore, I am afraid that no one, not even one so "gifted in the occult" as yourself (to quote your very own words), could expect anything but the cool welcome that always awaits uninvited visitors to Bleak Mountain. So do not come.

Very truly yours,

(signed)

Baroness Meen
Bleak Mountain

P.S. DO NOT COME.

"As you can see the Baroness hasn't exactly invited me," Herman admitted, putting the letter back in his suitcase. "But I think that won't matter too much once I actually arrive on her doorstep, do you?"

"*Are* you 'gifted in the occult'?" croaked the mouse.

"I believe I could be. That's almost the same thing,

don't you think? As of this moment I really don't know any magic at all but I'm sure I shall manage somehow to convince the Baroness that I do."

"You mean that you really plan to go to Bleak Mountain—*anyway*?"

"Of course."

"What for?" demanded Wallace.

"To study magic, of course."

"To study MAGIC!" shrieked Wallace, suddenly comprehending.

"You got it. Finally. It's my life's ambition. In spite of what the Baroness Meen said in her letter, I'm sure that I'll be able to convince her that she could use an apprentice."

"Another one?"

"You mean she has one already?"

"She has—oh, dear—MANGLE!" cried Wallace, remembering suddenly where he'd been headed when he encountered Herman. "I've got to go. I was on my way to warn Cynthia-Seven that Mangle might be in the forest. There's not a moment to lose." With that the mouse bounded off.

"Wait! Wait!" Herman called. "Won't you tell me the way to Bleak Mountain?"

"Follow me," yelled the mouse over his shoulder without slowing down in the slightest. "It's certain that you don't know much about witches. Cynthia-Seven will set you straight!"

2

What an excitable fellow, Herman thought as he struggled to keep up, his suitcase bumping against his shins. Wallace was quite a bit ahead in spite of the fact that the mouse often stumbled and fell in the deep snow.

So frequently had the mouse been prostrating himself in the deep snow that it was a minute or two before Herman realized that Wallace had disappeared completely.

"Wallace! Wallace! Where are you?" he called.

"Heeeeeeelp."

Herman looked all around but the mouse was nowhere in sight. "*Where* are you?"

"Down here," came a muffled reply.

In a moment Herman was peering down at Wallace. What a clumsy creature, he thought, but aloud he said: "At the rate you fall into holes and land upside down in snow drifts, I don't know how you managed before I came along."

He pulled the mouse out. "What a deep hole. What could have made it?"

Suddenly Wallace stiffened with fright. "MANGLE!" he breathed. "This hole had to be made by Mangle's iron boot. Mangle must be in the forest."

Iron boot? Who is Mangle? Herman was about to ask when he *saw* him!

A giant of gargantuan size, Mangle was silhouetted against the sky on the crest of the ridge beyond. Even from this distance Herman could see that the giant limped, swinging a great iron boot on his left foot in a wide arc.

Clump! CLUMP! Clump! CLUMP! Clump! CLUMP!

The uneven steps split the silence of the forest.

Clump! CLUMP! Clump! CLUMP! Clump! CLUMP!

Distorted and grotesque, the giant's face was permanently molded in anger. Deep furrows of rage pitted his wide forehead above deeply sunken eyes. His ears were bulbous and misshapen in sharp contrast to a small flat nose. Like his huge hands and feet, the giant's head was enormous—and hairless. Not a single bristle sprouted from his enormous stone-like head. Except that he moved, Mangle might have been an ancient gargoyle hewed out of rock.

For a moment they were frozen in their tracks. "Quick," whispered Herman, recovering first. He leaped behind a tree, pulling the unprotesting Wallace with him.

"Is he coming *this* way?" croaked Wallace.

They listened.

"I don't think so," Herman answered, peering around the tree cautiously. A great canvas bag was slung over the giant's shoulder. The bag lumped and swelled and trembled. "What's he carrying over his shoulder?"

"Oh," the mouse gasped. "That must be his catch for the Baroness' dinner."

The sound of the giant's footsteps grew fainter.

"He's going the other way. Let's go while we have the chance," said the mouse. "We have to warn Cynthia-Seven."

They ran as fast as they could. Finally, almost out of breath, Wallace threw himself down in the center of a small clearing. Herman sank at his side.

"Thank goodness we're in time. She hasn't gone out yet," declared Wallace with relief, observing the undisturbed snow. "CYNTHIA-SEVEN!" he bellowed in so loud a burst Herman's ears rang. "CYNTHIA-SEVEN!" the mouse roared again.

In spite of this thunderclap nothing happened. "Is she rather far away?" asked Herman. But just then the snow in front of them began to ripple and shake. Herman backed away from the percolating snow.

"Look!"

"I know," said the mouse calmly.

At that moment the snow before them erupted and a long pair of curly black rabbit ears popped up through the opening.

Could this be Cynthia-Seven, Herman wondered.

It was Cynthia-Seven, though all that could be seen of her were her ears, all curlicues of jet black fur, and two huge wide-set blue eyes.

What an enormous rabbit, thought Herman.

"This is Herman Lutt," announced Wallace.

"How do you do?" said Herman formally, tipping his cap.

"How nice, more company. Some of my nephews and nieces arrived yesterday," the rabbit responded, gesturing in the direction of her feet and revealing a very plump body indeed.

As if on cue, nine or ten furry little rabbits jumped out of the burrow. "Not now, dears. Go back and join the others. Auntie's talking now."

Immediately, the young rabbits dove down into the burrow but a lot of twittering and sniggering and squeals and *ouches* wafted up from below.

"Monroe-Four! Stop that this instant," Cynthia-Seven called down to them. "Agatha-Twenty-One and Matilda-Eight leave him alone."

More screeches and laughter and still louder *ouches* floated up.

"Please excuse me for a moment." The black roly-poly head disappeared.

"Why does everyone have a number after his name?"

"Everyone doesn't," answered Wallace. "Just rabbits."

"But why?"

"Because they have so many children and run out of names very quickly," Wallace continued in a bored tone. "They have to use names over and over. The first one to be called, say, Joseph, is just Joseph but the next Joseph is Joseph-Two and so on. It's quite simple," he concluded, confirming a very recent opinion that boys must be rather uninformed creatures indeed.

"Thank goodness my sister sent only twenty," said Cynthia-Seven sticking her head out of the burrow again. "I don't think I could have managed if she'd sent them all."

"Cynthia-Seven, I have to tell you something." Wallace glanced nervously about, striving for an even tone. "Mangle's in the forest. We've seen him."

Instantly, and this time without an "excuse me," the curly black head disappeared.

"She's terrified of Mangle," Wallace explained in a whisper. "As you may have noticed she's rather fa . . . er . . . ah . . . overweight so she'd make an especially good . . . ah . . . catch. We'll have to watch our words."

"Where did you see him?" floated up out of the burrow.

"On the other side of the forest. I believe we are safe here but you'd better send the young ones home while the coast is clear."

Instantly, an avalanche of young rabbits poured out of the burrow and all in a pack hopped wildly off.

Two blue eyes gleamed at them over the edge of the burrow.

"Wallace tells me that you can give me some information about Baroness Meen," said Herman stepping closer to Cynthia-Seven.

The eyes vanished.

"Hey! Take it easy," scolded the mouse. "She's very easily alarmed. Let me do the talking." He called down the burrow: "Don't worry, I'll protect you." Wallace turned and addressed Herman. "I'm quite tough, you know." He clenched his fists and thrust his jaw forward belligerently, admiring the image he cast in shadow on the snow.

Herman laughed.

"You don't think so, huh?" The mouse circled Herman and put up his paws like a boxer, encouraged by his elongated shadow.

"Of course, I do," Herman assured him, trying to be polite but having to stifle a smile behind his hand.

"I should say so! I may be short but nobody would dare to tangle with me," bragged the mouse. He feinted an uppercut and then a right jab with such force that he was spun around, his back now to Herman.

"Where did you go? Afraid of me, huh?" he chirped, making dreadful faces and swinging his fists wildly.

"Isn't he just brutal," said Cynthia-Seven proudly, reappearing again. "I feel so safe when Wallace's around." The furry rolls of fat shook with pleasure.

"Quite," agreed Herman, trying not to smile too broadly.

Soothed, the little pugilist studied Herman. "I guess you could be pretty tough yourself. Let's be friends. Shake."

Herman bent low and extended a finger to the mouse. Wallace shook it solemnly and then turned to Cynthia-Seven. "Herman needs our advice."

"That's right," said Herman. "I need directions to the Baroness Meen's castle on Bleak Mountain."

"You don't mean *to* her castle? You mean away *from*?"

"No I do mean *to* her castle as I hope to be her—"

"WHAT?" screeched the rabbit, clasping her chubby head in her paws.

"—apprentice."

Cynthia-Seven stared at Herman in disbelief. "But I thought that you had seen Mangle."

"What has he got to do with it?"

"Mangle is the Baroness' lackey. Here in the forest we are protected from the Baroness and Mangle by a wide river which surrounds the mountain like a moat. But in winter the river freezes over. When the ice is thick enough to hold his weight, Mangle can cross over into our forest to hunt."

Wallace shuddered even though he knew that neither the Baroness nor Mangle had a taste for mice.

"Well, it's true that I hadn't counted on Mangle but—"

"And besides Mangle to guard her, the witch has a long black snake which she lets roam about the castle freely."

"I hadn't counted on a snake either." Herman admitted.

"The snake smells of almonds and has hypnotic purple eyes," continued Cynthia-Seven.

"And if the snake looks at you—straight into your eyes, that is—you're paralyzed and can't run away," added Wallace, shuddering.

"So, I'm sure you have no intention now of going to Bleak Mountain to study with the Baroness," she said feeling satisfied that she had saved Herman from a dreadful fate.

"Oh, but I do," responded Herman. "I intend to go. Anyway."

3

B ut won't your parents be worried about you?" continued Cynthia-Seven, determined to stop Herman from going to Bleak Mountain.

"My parents died when I was a baby. Ever since I can remember I've lived in the orphanage. There are so many children at the orphanage that I doubt if anyone would even notice that I was missing."

"Were they unkind to you there?"

"No, though the other boys used to tease me because I said I was going to be famous when I grew up. And so I will be, if I can study with the Baroness."

"Study . . . with the Baroness? What does he mean, Wallace?" asked the rabbit, puzzled.

"Oh, he doesn't mean anything at all," said Wallace hoping to divert Herman from that subject.

But Herman kept on. "Who can explain a heart's desire to any heart but his own? Or, why someone must climb the Alps or why another gives up everything to become a painter or another sets out alone to chart unexplored places in the world? So how can I explain my own modest desire to study magic with the Baroness?"

"You mean you want to become a WITCH?" screeched Cynthia-Seven.

"I think I can learn a lot from the Baroness. Even her letter, written, I think, in ice is—"

"ICE!" Cynthia-Seven screamed so loudly this time that Herman's ears started to ring again. "THE ICE WITCH! Herman, you mustn't go to Bleak Mountain. The Baroness will turn *you* into ice!"

"Me? Into ice?" mumbled Herman, beginning to feel a little uncomfortable.

"She's called the Ice Witch because it's been said that she is so cold and unfeeling a person that anyone she looks upon turns into ice. We've heard that she wears a patch over one eye to keep the full force of her gaze from turning everything around her into ice."

"That's probably what she meant by the 'cool welcome' she promised you in her letter," affirmed Wallace. "I'd say she has a nasty sense of humor."

"But isn't there any way to avoid her gaze?"

"NONE!" cried Wallace and Cynthia-Seven in unison.

"Oh," said Herman. "To be turned into ice is a horrible fate. I think I could have dealt with Mangle and perhaps even the snake but how could I avoid the Baroness' gaze?"

"I'm very glad you have come to your senses at last." Cynthia-Seven expressed her joy by hugging Wallace so hard that the mouse couldn't catch his breath.

"I guess I'd better start back before it gets too dark," Herman said with a deep sigh.

"I know you must be disappointed but some difficulties are simply insurmountable. But don't worry, we'll escort you back through the forest," Cynthia-Seven volunteered, nudging Wallace soundly in the ribs.

"*We* could?" Wallace sputtered, still trying to catch his breath.

"Of course, we could."

"I suppose Herman might require directions back to where he started from," Wallace conceded grudgingly. "But, Cynthia-Seven, you couldn't possibly walk such a distance."

"Oh, I was hoping you'd suggest it, Wallace dear," said the rabbit.

"What?" asked Wallace, bewildered but still wary.

"You clever mouse," she continued. "So then it will be all right for me to ride on the sled. I'm sure Herman will be kind enough to help you to pull me. Won't you, Herman?"

"But what about *afterwards*?" protested Wallace, picturing the return trip without Herman.

As if she had just thought of it, Cynthia-Seven added: "There's a hill on the way to the village side of the forest. We would all take turns sliding down on the sled. Sledding always gives me such a good appetite."

The sled was a sleek affair of varnished maple wood set on sharp, polished runners. The rabbit was a huge mound sitting on top of Herman's suitcase strapped to the sled. She hummed to herself, confident that the effect of her new blue bow which matched her eyes would not be lost on Wallace.

The late afternoon wind was brisk and the surface of the snow had already frozen into a hard crust so the sled slid easily. While Herman pulled, Wallace pushed from the rear. At least he was supposed to be pushing. But from time to time he would step up on one of the shiny runners and glide effortlessly along—until his conscience bothered him. Then he would step down again and resume pushing. I really must reserve my strength for the trip back, he thought. Though how in the world he would ever manage to tow all that weight back through the forest by himself he really didn't know.

"Wonderful fun, isn't it?" Cynthia-Seven called to Wallace over her shoulder.

"First-rate," squeaked Wallace, hopping quickly down off the runner.

It wasn't long before the trio reached the summit of a steep hill whose far side was conveniently free of trees. Herman and Wallace gave the sled a gentle push and down the hill went Cynthia-Seven screeching with delight all the way to the bottom.

"Wait," Herman called. "I'll come down and bring the sled back up for Wallace." He was down the hill in a flash and was just about to drag the sled back up when a huge shadow fell between him and the sled. Frozen where he stood, Herman felt paralyzed as directly in front of him, its wide mouth open and drooling, was a bear.

From his vantage point at the top of the hill Wallace looked on in horror. He felt panic spread around his heart and travel icily down his legs. He tried to run. Not toward his helpless friends, but *away* from them. He couldn't help himself. In his mindless haste, he lost his balance completely and fell. In an instant he was rolling. Not away from the danger, but *toward* it!

Down he whirled, like a ball, gathering speed and snow. With each revolution, more and more snow clung to his fur. By the time he had spun mid-way down the hill, nothing could be seen of Wallace but his head and a pair of twitching feet sticking out of a gigantic snowball which grew bigger and bigger as it increased in speed.

Intent on the pair, the bear advanced with confidence. None of them saw or heard the giant sphere until the avalanche was nearly upon them. But then it was too late for the bear to leap aside. Its full force hit him squarely in the chest. Stunned, he fell in a heap. The impact threw Wallace, dizzy but otherwise unhurt, onto the sled.

Without a moment's hesitation, Herman took off dragging the sled with its two occupants behind him. On he plunged through the forest, slackening speed now and then only to check that both passengers were still aboard.

At times Herman imagined he saw huge bears with big teeth and twitching lips staring at him off in the distance that faded but then popped out again in another place. He ran until he was so breathless he couldn't take another step. He slumped down next to the sled and closed his eyes. When he opened them, he saw that only Cynthia-Seven was sitting on the sled atop his suitcase.

"Where's Wallace," he asked in alarm.

"We're all safe now thanks to you. Wallace is over there." The rabbit pointed. "Still walking in circles." Her rolls of fat shook with suppressed laughter. "He hasn't been able to stop. So much spinning. I am afraid poor Wallace has to unwind."

Sure enough, there was Wallace, racing in mad circles around them as if his feet were propelled by a will of their own. Already he had plowed a deep furrow in the snow.

"It is not the least bit funny," Wallace said, angrily. "You wouldn't think it was funny if it were you. Furthermore, I think I deserve a little more respect after what I did, saving you both at great personal risk," he fumed as he began yet another cycle around them.

Before he had completed two more full circles he had convinced himself that he was a hero. He even managed to take a few wide swings at an imaginary bear. But the unwinding took so much of his strength that he had to give that up, content to mutter under his breath, "Take that. And that. And THAT." But eventually Wallace's motor ran down, and he sank, gratefully, onto the snow.

"Herman, it is nearly dark. It is too late now for us to escort you to the edge of the forest. We'll have to take shelter for the night."

"There's a big hollow tree over there," said Wallace. "Herman and I can spend the night in it."

"Fine. Fortunately, my burrow's just beyond the rise over there. Pick me up early in the morning." And without waiting for an argument, Cynthia-Seven dashed off. "Sleep tight," she called.

4

"Tight" was exactly the right word for it, thought Herman when he awoke the next morning, stiff from spending the night in the cramped shelter of the hollow tree.

"I'd like to get an early start this morning if I am to get back to the orphanage by the afternoon," he said to Wallace as they set out for Cynthia-Seven's burrow, making fresh tracks in the smooth, new snow that had fallen during the night

"It's a good day to be going in the opposite direction from Bleak Mountain," observed Wallace, quite himself again, walking briskly and *straight*.

They were nearing Cynthia-Seven's burrow when they saw something blue flashing in the sunlight.

"Cynthia-Seven's bow! She must have dropped it here yesterday. She'll be glad to know that she hasn't lost it," said Wallace as he picked up the blue bow.

"Odd," mused Herman. "If Cynthia-Seven lost her bow yesterday, the snow that fell during the night would certainly have covered it up, don't you think?"

Wallace frowned. "Then perhaps she lost it when she came this way this morning."

"But we haven't passed her on the way—"

The same thought struck them both! They ran and soon reached the clearing where the rabbit had her burrow. Chills ran up and down their spines for here the snow was trampled and churned as if there had been a struggle. But worse—all about were the deep uneven footprints which could have been made by only one person. Mangle had returned!

"Cynthia-Seven" they both shouted over and over but there was no answer to their calls.

"It is true then," sobbed Wallace.

It was true. Cynthia-Seven had arisen very early that morning, taken her usual diet breakfast of raw carrots and lettuce, and had just started out to meet Wallace and Herman at the big hollow tree when she heard a familiar but terrifying sound.

Clump! CLUMP! Clump! CLUMP1! Clump! CLUMP!

She debated only a second: Was it better to try to run back to her burrow or should she hide under a tree?

In that fatal moment of hesitation, Mangle was upon her. His gargantuan hand closed over her head. He held her up painfully by the ears knocking her blue bow to the ground.

"Nice 'n plump," he observed as he poked her in the ribs.

It was useless to scream but she did anyway.

For a very long time.

As he trudged back through the forest, Mangle, who considered himself something of a poet though he certainly could have benefited from some lessons in prosody, sang loudly:

> "A fat young rabbit have I.
> But a fatter rabbit will I
> Cook in spices and potatoes
> And serve on a bed of tomatoes.
>
> I'll fatten her up
> For the Baroness' sup.
> Rabbit stew! Rabbit stew!
> Rabbit stew!"

The downcast pair waited well into the afternoon. But finally there was no denying the truth. *Cynthia-Seven would not return!*

"It's my fault Cynthia-Seven was captured," said Herman sadly. "She wanted to escort me to the edge of the forest and . . ." his voice broke.

"If only there were something we could do," wailed the mouse.

Herman kicked at the snow with the stub of his shoe. Then he looked Wallace straight in the eyes. "There *is* something."

"What? What?"

"We could rescue her," Herman said recklessly, his stomach dropping at his own words.

Wallace gasped. "You mean . . . ?"

"We must go at once. There is no time to lose."

"Let's think first," Wallace cautioned. "We can't go without some sort of a plan."

So they thought. And thought. But neither of them could come up with a plan.

Herman paced up and down. Wallace clenched and unclenched his fists.

"Thinking is useless," Herman announced after a while. "We'll have to go . . . without a plan!"

5

In the afternoon light the snow glinted eerily. Tossing and clacking upon themselves in the wind, the icy branches of the trees gave off a melancholy toneless refrain.

Herman was very worried. What has come over me, he thought gloomily, to make me think that with the aid of a mere field mouse I could rescue Cynthia-Seven from under the noses of both the Baroness Meen and Mangle, not to mention the dreadful snake. Now trudging through the forest toward the witch's castle, his suitcase bumping painfully against his already sore ankles, Herman regretted his impulsiveness. Yet, he couldn't shake a feeling of guilt. Hadn't Cynthia-Seven left the shelter of her own safe burrow in order to help him? Wasn't he, therefore, responsible? Wasn't it up to him to save her?

"We've come deeper into the forest than I have ever been before," offered Wallace, interrupting Herman's ruminations. The mouse had been uncharacteristically silent for some time.

"I don't suppose we'll run into too many difficulties until we reach the castle," Herman said as cheerfully as he was able. The silence was getting him down.

"Difficulties?" Wallace repeated and then grew quiet again.

Difficulties! That's putting it mildly, Herman thought. Mangle was scarcely what he would term a mere difficulty. As for the snake, he decided not to think about it at all. But how would they gain entrance to the castle without being detected? Neither he nor Wallace had any idea of the layout of the castle assuming they could gain entrance. Where would they hide in the castle while they searched for Cynthia-Seven? How long might it take to find her? Or—the thought was appalling—would they be *in time*!

"You don't think Cynthia-Seven is in any immediate danger, do you, Herman?" Wallace piped up suddenly as if he had been sharing Herman's thoughts.

They stared at each other, the unspoken horror foremost in their minds. Finally, with considerable effort, Wallace spoke: "I think that Mangle will want to fatten her up ...even more. I've heard that the Baroness is very thin but that she likes only the plumpest, the fattest of . . . " He was unable to finish his sentence. They quickened their pace.

But Herman couldn't stop thinking. How would they manage to escape the Baroness' gaze? But, what if—the idea was worth clinging to—what if the Baroness were not at all as Wallace and Cynthia-Seven had described her. After all, wasn't she a witch? He found the thought comforting. But what if—what if the Baroness were not as dreadful as they had said—what if she were *worse*!

They walked for what seemed like miles, pausing only to snatch a few wild berries off bushes as they passed, or to scoop up handfuls of snow to quench their thirst.

Then abruptly the forest thinned out.

"We must be close to the river," murmured Wallace with mixed feelings.

In the next moment the frozen river lay before them. On the far side, Bleak Mountain rose up straight up into the sky, its peak lost in the clouds. A mammoth mass of rock studded with withered trees, the mountain seemed bereft of all life. Below, at its base, the river girdled the mountain like a medieval moat.

For several moments the two rescuers gazed upward in silence.

"I've heard that her castle is at the very peak."

"Then it will be a tough climb. So let's get started," Herman said with a determination that surprised even him. Gingerly, he stepped onto the frozen river. It held his weight.

"Come on, Wallace."

They were a little more than halfway across when they heard a loud creak.

"What's that?"

Suddenly a crazed line streaked under their feet.

"The ice is cracking!" Wallace yowled.

They charged forward. The crease followed, twisting and zigzagging under their feet like a rope come alive.

"Faster!" Herman yelled. "We can make it to the other side."

Just as the ice buckled under them, Herman grabbed Wallace and with a terrific lunge attained the bank.

They were on Bleak Mountain!

They turned to watch as the ice continued to break up. In the next moment the river became a raging swell filled with jagged blocks of ice which bobbled and dipped like apples in a tub as the current swept them downstream.

Herman and Wallace stared at the river. Now, there could be no turning back!

The mouse was standing a little apart from Herman on the edge of the bank, watching sadly as the swirling water cut off their only return route, when the ground collapsed under him.

He hit the icy water screaming. The water surged over him as the current pulled him downstream.

"Swim, Wallace. Swim. This way!" Herman raced along the bank.

The mouse fought against the pull of the current. Jagged chunks of ice bobbled in the water around him. He tried to seize one but it was too slippery. Just when he knew that the icy water and the strength of the river were too much for him, he was thrown against something sharp. A root protruded out from the side of the bank, just above the water line. He grabbed for it. And got it.

Then two strong arms lifted him out of the freezing water.

"Wallace! Wallace! Are you all right?" whispered Herman trying to keep the fear out of his voice.

But Wallace's teeth were chattering so uncontrollably he couldn't answer. His whole body shook. His fur, matted and bunched, had already, in places, hardened into icicles.

"I'll build a fire to dry you off," said Herman.

When the small fire was at last crackling, Wallace managed to stammer in spite of his shivers: "I'mmmmm . . . fffffffffine . . . nnnnow."

They sat in silence but they both were wondering what could go wrong next.

"There's no moon tonight. I'm glad we have a fire," said Herman but his eyes, darting to and fro warily, belied his words. "Get some sleep, Wallace. I'll keep watch," he said, knowing that if Mangle were still wandering over the mountainside the giant would see their fire.

6

Wallace awoke the next morning with a dreadful cold. Yet the fact that they had survived a night on Bleak Mountain gave the pair renewed courage.

"We bedda ged going," Wallace said, quite nasally.

Their ascent was slow and arduous. The mountainside was practically a sheer upward rise. A small boulder, dislodged by Herman's foot, went crashing down the mountain. They heard it breaking and tearing through the trees for a long time.

"We must be very high up," said Herman.

They looked down. Far below, the river seemed like a silver thread.

"Led's rest now," pleaded Wallace, coughing and sniffling.

"All right," agreed Herman. "Over here." He indicated a large tree which they could lean against.

But as soon as they sat down: ZING! A heavy canvas bag dropped from the branch above plunging them into darkness. Then *SWOOSH!* The bag containing the terrified friends was hoisted high into the air. They hung there, trapped.

"We must be in one of Mangle's trabs," cried Wallace.

The bag swayed as they scrambled to find foot room on its soft, yielding bottom. Herman nearly stepped on Wallace in an attempt to climb to the top. He clawed at the gathered edges. But the rope was knotted firmly on the outside.

"Is dere noding we can do?" wailed Wallace.

They waited in darkness, listening to the sound of the wind and the creaking of the rope.

"Wallace," Herman said after a while, "I'm not sorry we came."

"I'm nod either. Poor Cynthia-Seven. Whad will happen to her now?"

"I don't think I would mind this fate half so much if I knew that she was safe and—"

"—I've god an idea," Wallace exclaimed. "I might be able to chew a hole in this cloth. Id's worth a try!"

At once the mouse set about nibbling furiously at a corner of the bag.

"How's it going?" Herman asked after a while.

"Don't interrupt," said Wallace testily, spitting out a few threads.

But before Wallace could resume his efforts, they heard footsteps. Approaching. Near. Nearer.

The trapper has come to claim his catch, Herman thought in panic.

They heard his breathing and his clothing rustle faintly in the wind. They felt his hand jostle the bag making it swing wildly. They heard the scratch of a knife on canvas. In the next instant the knife stabbed downward, splitting the cloth, flooding the inside with light and spilling them onto the ground.

"Are you all right"'" asked the roundest little old man they had ever seen. He wore a hooded white cloak like woven snow.

It took the pair a moment to realize that they were rescued. Herman recovered first. "Oh, yes, we're fine. Thank you. Thank you."

"It's lucky that I happened along. Whenever I come upon one of Mangle's traps, I spring it. But this is the first time I freed a creature like you. What are you doing on Bleak Mountain?"

But before either of the relieved pair could answer, a familiar but terrifying sound resounded not very far away.

Clump! CLUMP! Clump! CLUMP! Clump! CLUMP!

"It's Mangle. He must be coming to inspect his trap!" cried the old man.

"Where can we hide?" squeaked Wallace. He looked about frantically for cover but there was no place for concealment.

Clump! CLUMP! Clump! CLUMP! Clump! CLUMP!

"Quick with you now," the old man directed. "Get inside my cloak. It will make us invisible."

"No!" gasped Wallace, flinching. "Led's run for id, Herman."

"No time now," said the old man. "Into my pocket with you." He scooped up the mouse and slipped him gently into the outside breast pocket of his cloak. Then he drew Herman and his suitcase within the folds of his cloak, pulling the hood down over his face. He was fastening the last button as Mangle came into view.

The giant made straight for his trap. He walked right past the trembling trio! Are we really invisible, wondered Herman as he peeked at the giant through the narrow slit of a buttonhole.

When Mangle saw that his trap had been ripped open and was empty, he grew exceedingly angry. He snatched the torn bag down from the branch and stamped on it. The giant vented his rage on the mountain itself. He kicked at the snow, digging out great divots of earth with his iron boot. He wrenched a small nearby spruce tree out the ground. Breaking it in half over his colossal knees, he trampled the branches into pieces, roaring his fury into the wind. Momentarily winded, he stopped to recover. At that moment Wallace sneezed.

The giant whirled around. He stared steadily at the very spot where the trio stood trembling and holding their breaths. He stepped closer. Closer still. Another step. Herman thought he would faint. Then the giant walked right past them!

For a long time they could hear the giant stomping over the mountainside, ripping and tearing as he went. Finally, when they could no longer hear him, the little old man opened his cloak.

"How can we ever thank you for saving our lives twice?"

"Twice?" said the old man, puzzled. "What do you mean 'twice'? Oh, now I remember … Mangle's trap," he mumbled absently. "Very glad to be of help—just in the nick of time as it turned out."

"And what a wonderful cloak."

"Is it a magic cloak? Are you a WITCH?" Wallace popped out of the pocket of the cloak and started to back away.

"Oh, are you?" Herman asked, delighted at the prospect.

"A witch? Me? No, no. Whatever gave you that idea?"

"Thank goodness for that," said Wallace, but still on his guard.

"For what?" asked the old man scratching his head.

What an absent-minded old fellow, thought Herman but he was much too grateful to say so. "I'm Herman Lutt and this is Wallace."

"How-do-you-do? Zachery Tack at your service. Now that we are properly introduced, let's be off while all's clear."

"Where to?" asked Wallace rather sharply.

"To my house, of course. You could probably use a hot meal and a warm fire, couldn't you?"

7

Zachery Tack led them around to the other side of the mountain to a path which was little more than a narrow ledge winding around the other side of the mountain.

Wallace and Herman looked down.

It was a sheer drop straight down.

They looked up.

The mountainside was smooth stone all the way up.

"Few people would ever think to use this path," explained the little old man, noting their hesitation, "but it works well for me. Come along. Don't be afraid."

They crept along cautiously, inching their way in silence, except for an occasional squeak from Wallace when the mouse skidded on a icy patch.

"Not much farther," Zachery Tack reassured them.

Sure enough, at the next turn they came to a door painted a brilliant orange, trimmed in green.

"Come in," beckoned the old man, stepping aside to allow them to pass inside ahead of him.

They entered a most unusual room. All the walls were covered, floor to ceiling, with shelf upon shelf, row upon row, of glass containers of all sizes and shapes and hues imaginable. There were thousands of bottles and vessels and cisterns and beakers and decanters and phials and jars. Each held a brightly colored liquid. A network of laboratory bottles connected by tubes and glass pipes zigzagged across the ceiling. Through this an amber liquid dripped and bubbled. The tubes crisscrossed down to a number of copper vats, and then up again to the main pipeline where they joined other tanks and containers until there was very little headroom. Herman had to duck his head for fear of jarring the entire apparatus.

At the back of the room a large pot-bellied stove snapped and crackled invitingly. They had already stepped toward the warmth of the stove and Zachery Tack had already closed the door when Wallace saw the *cats!* Scores and scores of them suddenly advanced from behind every conceivable nook and cranny. Large tabbies, jet blacks, Maltese, grey-striped, tri-coloreds, Persians, pure whites, Manx, Angoras, hordes of tiny fluffy kittens, Siamese with large crossed blue eyes, calicos and even tortoise-shells—each wearing a cluster of tiny silver bells around their necks.

The chiming was deafening when the cats spied Wallace.

"Don't be afraid, Wallace," said Zachery Tack. "They won't hurt you. Quiet now, my dears." Immediately the din ceased and all of the cats sat down.

"Are you SURE?" Wallace snapped, stepping behind Herman all the same.

"Sure of what? Oh, yes, the cats. I am a bit absent-minded at times. Yes, yes. I am very sure that not one of my precious dears will hurt you. Quite sure. Sit down. Lunch is will be ready very soon."

At once the little old man busied himself with pots and pans and sauces and seasonings until the two hungry wayfarers were drooling in anticipation.

"You must be a wizard," said Herman by way of praise as he pushed his empty plate away when he had finished. "That was a really wonderful meal."

"How did you guess?" replied Zachery Tack, wiping his mouth on his shirt sleeve.

"Whad?" asked Wallace, immediately ceasing to chew.

"That I am a wizard."

"*You are?*" chorused the pair.

"Yes, a wizard—of sorts as I'm so forgetful these days. But at the risk of immodesty, I must admit that I do have a few talents. My white cloak for instance. Yet, it looks so much like a mound of snow that I sometimes wonder if the cloak really makes me invisible or just camouflages me," Zachery Tack said.

"Do you know the Baroness Meen?" asked Herman.

At once all the cats began to howl and growl and spit so loudly that the thousands of bottles on the shelves began to shake and jiggle.

"I'd rather that you wouldn't mention *her* name around here. As you can hear, it has a rather unsettling effect. Quiet, my darlings." At once the cats were silent.

"We're on our way to her castle," Wallace announced.

"You are?" exclaimed the wizard. It was his turn to gasp.

The two travelers poured out the full story of why Herman had come into the forest, Cynthia-Seven's capture and the arduous journey that had led them this far.

"How are you going to manage it?" asked the wizard, frowning.

There was a very uncomfortable silence.

"We're not sure yet," admitted Herman. "We came without a plan."

"My word," marveled the wizard. "Without a plan. You know about her pet snake."

"Yes," answered Wallace grimly, without turning his head toward Zachery Tack as he was concentrating on trying to stare down a rather large yellow tabby which had not taken its eyes off him since he had arrived.

"Oh, then you must also know about her gaze, no doubt."

"Yes, we do bud we must save Cynthia-Seven," wailed Wallace.

"Perhaps I can help you," mused the wizard, sympathetically.

"Would you?" they shouted together.

"Would I what?" asked the old man, again losing the thread of the conversation.

"Help us!" screeched the two in unison again.

"Well, let me see now," he muttered. "I don't know if I can remember where . . ." The wizard got up and began to browse through the labels on the thousands of bottles on the shelves. "Flea powder … no, that's certainly not it. More flea powder. I do need a lot of that, you know. Molasses … no … no. Ah! Here's what I'm looking for."

The wizard held up a bottle which contained a small quantity of thick blue syrup. "The very thing but there's only a little left. Just enough for one spoonful for each of you."

"Well, I don't know," said Herman, looking at the bottle the wizard held up to the light.

"This should protect you from her gaze—if you should actually confront her, which I hope you don't."

"How does it work?"

"That's not important. If you have confidence in something, you can accomplish wonders. But even confidence won't last forever. I'd say you'll have about twenty-four hours. Open wide," the wizard instructed.

The syrup inside the bottle glowed blue as a sapphire.

"No way!" protested Wallace, through clenched teeth. "Noding could induce me to swallow anything blue. Besides, I don't need id. We plan to enter the castle *undetected*."

They might never have convinced Wallace to open his mouth except that the large yellow tabby had stealthily approached until he was standing behind Wallace. Curious about the mouse, the tabby had put a tentative paw on Wallace's tail.

"YOW!" Wallace shrieked and, in that instant, Zachery Tack popped the spoon into the mouse's open mouth.

"Hey, that's petty good though *awfully* spicy," admitted Wallace in astonishment. It's making me sweat."

"Me, too," Herman said, licking his burning lips.

"Remember, you will be protected for only twenty-four hours," said Zachery Tack holding the bottle so they couldn't see the label: *Extra, Extra Red Hot Peppers In Blueberry Juice.*

"We must go now as every second counts."

The wizard waved good-bye from the door.

"Good-bye and thank you," the pair called from the path.

"Good luck," Zachery Tack called after them and then, closing the door, forgot them both immediately.

8

It was almost dark by the time Herman and Wallace could resume their ascent. Darkness brought a haze over the mountain. In the fog the trees, shrubs and rocks looked sinister and unnatural. A chilling wind whined through the trees and echoed down the mountainside like a moan but both Herman and Wallace still felt the effects of Zachery Tack's potion and were warm as toast.

"What is thad sound?" Wallace whispered.

"The wind, I think."

The moon appeared from behind a cloud and turned the fog into a smoky mist. A wolf howled somewhere in the distance. Occasional shafts of moonlight stabbing down between the gnarled branches lit a path in the blackness and they followed it. Coming around the trunk of a tree, Herman mistook the dark form of his own shadow for an approaching specter. When he had regained his breath, he laughed at himself. Am I afraid of my own shadow? But his laughter sounded false and hollow in the night air.

Finally, above them in the gloom they saw the fog-dulled lights of the Baroness Meen's castle.

"Come on. Let's hurry. We're almost there."

At last they reached the summit. There, haloed in the eerie mist, stood the castle. It was more like a fort, built of great blocks of rough grey granite. Almost a box, the castle's squareness was relieved only by one narrow turret, a tower which rose high into the clouds. Surrounding the castle was a high stone wall.

They circled the wall and soon found the entrance, two massive wooden gates held together by a heavy metal chain.

"What will we do now?" asked Wallace.

As if in answer a sudden blast of wind parted the gates slightly but just enough to allow Herman, dragging the mouse with him, to slip through the narrow opening.

Was that a convenient wind or have we stepped into a trap? Herman wondered just as an ancient quavering voice rang out:

"Herman Lutt, I presume. So you have come anyway."

There, in the castle doorway, stood the Baroness Mean with Mangle at her side. Before either of them could spy him in the darkness, Wallace leaped into Herman's jacket pocket and pulled the flap over his head.

Herman faced the Baroness alone.

The Baroness was all that legend had made her out to be. If it had been said that she was ugly, she was hideous. Her mouth, shaped by cruelty and selfishness, twisted with fury as she glared at him. Hers was a face that had never smiled except to ridicule. As if electrified, her silver hair stood straight out from her head. Tall and bony, she had such white skin that she seemed inhuman. The effect was numbing.

Herman was relieved to see that she wore a black patch over her right eye.   Bravely, he stepped forward. Through his jacket, he could feel Wallace trembling.

"Why do you insist on this visit?" thundered the Baroness. At her side, Mangle, ever the bully, sneered down at him.

"I couldn't resist, Baroness, since your fame has spread far and wide." Herman lifted his cap politely and bowed gallantly

"So you thought you could face my cool welcome?" she snarled.

Herman tried to seem taller by standing up on his toes. "I thought I might be able to thaw out any cool welcome," he said, tying to brazen it out as this seemed the only course open to him. He doffed his cap and bowed low again.

"Oh, did you?" roared the witch and with that she tore off the eye patch and looked straight at Herman.

A white flash streaked across the distance between them. Instantly, the ground was covered with a powdery white frost, like a dusting of fresh snow. Ice formed on the edges of Herman's coat shoulders. Frigid air passed over him like an icy wind but he felt quite warm though the end of his nose was rather cold.

A muffled voice, wavering but joyous, rose from the recesses of pocket: "It worked! The potion worked!"

"What's this? Not turned to ice?" screeched the Baroness, poking Mangle brutally in the ribs as if she blamed him.

"Your magic doesn't work against *me*," said Herman boldly, his courage returning. He gave silent thanks to Zachery Tack.

"Who are you?" asked the awed witch.

"I'm . . . er . . . a magician . . . a *powerful* magician. Your powers are useless on me." He felt a kick in the ribs as Wallace was trying to keep him from taking his bravado too far.

"What? No power over you?" The Baroness turned purple with rage. "How can this be?" she asked, replacing her eye patch now.

"Does one sorcerer tell his secrets to another sorcerer?" Herman said tauntingly, smiling broadly.

Another tiny kick.

"Come in then. It will be very amusing, I think, to find out which of us is the more powerful. Won't it, Mangle? Take his suitcase."

Inside the castle, Herman found himself in a tremendous chamber. Leading off this huge foyer were scores and scores of archways and doors. Oh, Cynthia-Seven, how will we ever find you in this maze?

9

You're trembling, I think," said the Baroness, placing a bony hand on Herman's shoulder. In spite of Herman's brave front, the witch sensed his underlying fear.

"I always tremble," responded Herman cleverly, "when I think how sad it will be to leave a place. You see, even though I've just arrived, I won't be able to stay here too long."

"Quite the contrary, my dear boy. I *now* hope you will be able to stay ever so long," said the witch smiling grotesquely.

"Oh . . . how . . . kind. 'Ever so long' did you say."

"Yes. Ever so long."

"Oh," said Herman again.

"I hate to disappoint you but I must tell you now that I shan't be around very much of the time."

"Oh, not much of the time? What a pity," exclaimed Herman, relieved.

"Because of my duties around and about," explained the Baroness.

"I'd rather spend time you, of course. I am very disappointed," replied Herman, beginning to feel almost at ease.

"I thought you might *say* that. I might not be able to have supper with you for that same reason," said the Baroness pressing her advantage.

"Not dine with me?" repeated Herman, relieved though he hadn't considered the gruesome possibility before. "Of course, I'll miss your presence at dinner."

"I *knew* you would say that, too. Of course, I don't mean tonight. Tonight I *will* be able to dine with you," said the witch triumphantly.

"OH! OH! You will? Tonight. Oh, . . ." He was appalled. "How . . . nice," he managed at last, rewarding the Baroness with a grimace meant to be a smile.

The witch opened her mouth wide and emitted a sound like that of a chair being scrapped across a floor, which was her way of laughing. "Until dinner then . . . at nine. Mangle, show Herman Lutt to his room."

There will be some doing to this, thought Herman as Mangle, casting contemptuous glances down at him, led the way through one of scores of archways to a wide, steep stone staircase.

"Until nine," Mangle boomed as he closed the bedchamber door behind Herman. The clang of his iron boot echoed loudly on the stone floor as he limped down the long corridor.

Herman took his first real look at the room assigned to him. Except for the blanketed bed in the center of the chamber, nothing else suggested repose or slumber. For one thing the room was immense. The ceiling was domed. Floor to ceiling casement windows lined two walls. The glass panes rattled and creaked ominously.

Drafts assailed him from every direction. The floor and two remaining walls were stone and freezing to the touch. When Herman sagged against it, the bed gave off a cloud of dust and a dank musty odor.

"Is da coast clear?" Wallace whispered, peeking sheepishly out of Herman's pocket as the last echoing clang of Mangle's steps died away.

Herman turned his jacket inside out and shook Wallace onto the bed.

"I suppose you think I was afraid," said the mouse.

Herman didn't answer.

"Well, I wasn't. I was simply being practical. *One* of us had to keeb his wits about him and keeb hidden," the mouse insisted, still nasal. "What if she had seen us both? Den where would we be?"

"I can't see how things would be much different," said Herman testily.

"Well, *I* certainly can."

The wind moaned louder against the windows panes.

"Couldn't we sneak out right now and look for a bedda place to hide. It's absolutely freezing in this room. My cold could turn into pneumonia in a place like this."

"How could *we* do that?" Herman snapped, his temper a bit frayed. "Although they don't know *you're* here, they certainly know that *I* am. They'd start searching for me as soon as they discovered that I'd gone. Furthermore, it is much better to appear assured if we're to carry this off."

"I never expected this turn of events," wailed Wallace. "I thought we'd somehow find a secret passage into the castle, find Cynthia-Seven and leave the same way and never even see the Baroness. Or Mangle."

The mouse was now perched on the edge of Herman's suitcase and suddenly noticed that the inside lid was a mirror. Other than in rain puddles, Wallace had never seen his own reflection and it enthralled him.

"But the fact remains," Herman said irritably, "that we have seen her. Or, more importantly that she's seen *me*. So concentrate on thinking of something that fits the situation we're actually in."

"We're powerless against da witch. Even the potion Zachery Tack gave us will wear off some time tomorrow. It was foolish to come dere," the mouse moaned unfairly. "We can do nothing to help Cynthia-Seven. Noding." Despite his despair, Wallace studied his reflection with satisfaction.

"Well, I wish we had a plan. Any kind of plan. To think that my heart's desire has led us all to this," said Herman remorsefully.

Seeing Herman's distress, Wallace was sorry he had been angry. "I want to tell you, Herman, that I thought you were very brave with the Baroness. Very brave."

Herman was about to thank Wallace for his words of praise, when there was a loud knock on the door.

"Don't open it!" hissed Wallace, looking frantically about for a place to hide.

"Nine o'clock," came the now familiar booming voice of the giant through the door.

"Nine o'clock already! What shall I do?" whispered Herman.

"I'm not going to stay here all alone. I'm going with you!" With that, the mouse leaped back into Herman's jacket pocket.

In the next instant the door opened. "Follow me," the giant commanded.

All the way down the stairs with the pocketed Wallace bumping awkwardly against his side, Herman mustered his courage for the ordeal ahead. Though he was not in a mood to admit it to Wallace, it was comforting to know that the mouse was with him.

"In there," growled Mangle as he ushered Herman through one of the numerous archways and into the witch's dining room.

Herman was aware at once that the air smelled faintly of almonds. He wondered what the Baroness would be serving for dinner. In the center of the great room was a long marble table at which some thirty guests might have been seated quite comfortably. He saw that tonight there was a place setting at both ends of the long table. A very uncozy dinner for two! On the walls were stretched skins of bears, foxes, wolves as well as squirrels, raccoons and *rabbits*. It was a terrible reminder.

The Baroness Meen swept into the room and sat at the head of the table. She gestured to Herman to take the seat at the far end of the long table. An arrangement of candles in the center of the table provided the only illumination. But the faint light could not hide the witch's ugliness.

Bright red rouge had been applied too generously to her sunken cheeks. A dark mauve lipstick, drawn far beyond her own lip line covered half of the area above her mouth as well as much of her chin. Blue mascara dripped thickly from the ends of her lashes framing her one visible eye. The black eye patch covered her other eye. Smeared over her entire prune-like face was a thick coating of pink powder.

Herman slipped into his seat with as much assurance as he could manage. Immediately, Mangle served the first course, a thick, light green broth. The Baroness ate with gusto, emitting loud, greedy slurps. She finished well ahead of Herman who had some difficulty in swallowing his soup under the constant gaze of Mangle who stood directly behind his chair.

Thoughtfully, toying with something in her lap, the Baroness watched Herman who now had even more difficulty swallowing under the direct gaze of the witch.

"It's puree of Japanese beetles," she said abruptly.

"Beetles!" exclaimed Herman, his spoon arrested mid-way to his lips.

Mangle half-suppressed a giggle which sounded like someone being strangled.

"My favorite soup. I do hope you are enjoying it."

Writhing under the steady and penetrating stare on the back of his neck, Herman was about to attempt to answer the Baroness when slowly, gracefully, a small black head rose up from the witch's lap followed by a long, rope-like body. The black head swayed back and forth close to the Baroness' face. At the same moment Wallace peeked out from under the pocket flap. The witch did not notice the mouse but when the snake saw Wallace, it practically smiled.

Through the cloth of his coat, Herman felt Wallace flopping about in his pocket.

"My pet," the Baroness explained unnecessarily as the snake uncoiled itself a little more. "You're not alarmed, are you?"

Herman shook his head, a little too wildly.

"She smells quite lovely, doesn't she? She's shined with almond oil every day." The witch stared into the snake's hooded purple eyes.

Herman remembered the warning not to look the snake directly in the eyes but he needn't have concerned himself as all throughout the long dinner the Baroness ate greedily and noisily and all throughout dinner the snake never took its eyes from Herman's pocket.

Dessert was a quivering gelatinous black pudding.

"What is this amazing dish?" Herman asked before he put his spoon into his bowl.

"Blood pudding. Very tasty."

Herman carefully laid his spoon down on the table.

"Where did you learn magic?" demanded the Baroness abruptly.

"In India," Herman returned recklessly. "I studied with a swami," he added, carried away.

"Really! How very interesting," said the Baroness in a tone Herman couldn't interpret.

"Easy does it" came a whisper from the deep recesses of his pocket accompanied by a tiny kick.

"Indeed, yes," continued Herman, ignoring the mouse. "I studied for years and years. In fact, I earned a brown belt in black magic."

"Are you really immune to the magic of others?" asked the Baroness with false indifference.

"Of course," Herman said attempting to feint a yawn.

"Don't over do it" was punctuated with another kick.

"Can you do this?" With a snap of her bony fingers a great wind suddenly swirled over the table and extinguished the candles. "Can you?" she demanded over the roar of the wind.

"Of course," gulped Herman, straining to see in the darkness as the wind ruffled his hair.

SNAP! went the Baroness' fingers again and immediately the wind subsided. Mangle relit the candles and to Herman's relief then left the room.

"Can you *indeed*," roared the Baroness. "What about *this?*"

Thunder broke directly over Herman's head. Crackling streaks of lightning zigzagged around him. Then the jagged flashes of electricity rolled together into one ball and came to rest over Herman's head. The ball glowed like white hot silver. It gave off an immense heat.

"How boring all this is," replied Herman, sweat trickled down his neck into his shirt collar. "If you feel that you have to impress me, Baroness, you are just wasting your energy. I learned all that in my first year. Those are just parlor tricks."

The Baroness extinguished the ball of glowing sparks. "Is that so!" she hissed with smothered fury. "Then perhaps you'll show me what you have learned?"

"Certainly. Be glad to."

"Well?"

"Sometime, when I'm in the mood."

Just then the snake started to crawl down the table toward Herman, its eyes riveted on his pocket. "My snake seems fascinated by something about you," observed the Baroness, drawing the snake back to her.

Inside the pocket Wallace fell into a coughing spasm. Herman was forced to fake a few coughs to cover the sound.

"My, but you look exceptional – cough –cough –in this candlelight –cough," he said, hoping to divert her attention.

"Oh, do you think so," exclaimed the Baroness with surprise.

"I certainly do. As a matter of fact, I was . . . ah . . . struck by your ... ah ... appearance the first time I saw you. Surely you are aware of how your looks impress others."

The witch stroked a wart on her cheek, completely absorbed in the turn the conversation had now taken.

"I would have mentioned it much earlier but I didn't want to be, well, impertinent," continued Herman, smiling as broadly as he could manage. "You might have considered me very impertinent if I told you what a . . . ah . . . ah . . . rare creature you are."

"Impertinent? Impertinent? Goodness, no," crooned the witch. "Do go on."

"Well, in that case,' said Herman, who was now thoroughly enjoying the feeling of having the upper hand, "I do want to say that I consider you to be a rare, yes, a very rare creature indeed. But I know you are not interested in compliments."

"Compliments? Of course, not. I am above such things," said the Baroness, her tone of disappointment belying her words. "I am not at all interested in what people say but, of course, I would value *your* opinion, dear boy."

"I am a bit of a connoisseur having traveled and all that. India and so forth." Another tiny kick. "I hate to brag but I've seen a few charmers in my time." He attempted a rakish laugh.

"Charmers!" exclaimed the witch, taking the word to apply to herself but missing the pun.

"Yes, and your pet suits you so well." He said quickly as the snake had again uncoiled itself and was crawling down the long table toward him, its purple eyes glued on his jacket pocket.

The reminder worked. The Baroness reached out and hauled the escaping snake back to her.

"Go on," she urged. "An unusual pet. So uncommon. Like you, dear lady."

"I don't know when I've met someone as clever as you and one so young, too," she crooned, grinning coyly and rolling her one visible eye at him. "I could listen to you forever."

"Well, not forever, of course. As I won't be able to stay forever."

"Why not? You *could*."

"Really, I *couldn't*."

An exchange of "coulds" and "couldn'ts" might have continued indefinitely but Mangle reentered the dining room. He whispered something in the Baroness' ear. She rose quickly, still cradling the snake in her arms.

Herman rose abruptly too. Too abruptly. His glass of milk tumbled over, spilling down the front of his jacket.

"Not to worry," exclaimed the Baroness. "Mangle will clean it for you in the kitchen. You'll have it back in the morning good as new."

"NO! NO!" screamed Herman as his pocket thumped wildly against his side. "I wouldn't think of troubling Mangle. It's a mere nothing. An old jacket—"

His voice broke off ineffectually as he was nearly hoisted off the ground by his arms. Before he could stop him, Mangle had deftly peeled off his jacket and was holding it high over his head.

"NO! NO!" Herman shrieked. In his panic, he tried to grab the jacket out of Mangle's hands.

"Is there something in your jacket that you want?"

Five eyes turned on Herman expectantly.

"Yes! I mean, ah . . . no," he stammered. What could he do? He could never manage to slip Wallace out of his jacket pocket without being seen. How he wished he *were* a magician!

"Are you sure?" demanded the witch, casting a searching look upon him.

There was nothing Herman could say as Mangle carried Wallace off to the kitchen inside his jacket pocket.

10

The kitchen was the warmest room in the Baroness Meen's castle. There were two reasons for this. It was the only chamber in the stone castle which had no windows and, thus, had no chilling drafts to sweep suddenly over one's feet or to nestle icily between one's shoulder blades. Second, a great fire always raged in the open hearth pit in the center of the room. It was here on a spit or in the deep brick oven above the hearth that Mangle prepared all the Baroness' meals.

Actually the kitchen was quite cozy. Overhead, myriad copper pots and pans of all sizes dangled from metal hooks in the ceiling. Along the walls jars and bottles of colorful dried seasonings lined the shelves: mustard, nutmeg, pepper, anise, basil, turmeric, ginger, salt, thyme, sage, paprika, oregano, cinnamon, dill, cayenne, mint, marjoram, rosemary, tarragon, fennel, savory, sesame, sorrel, saffron, bay leaves, cloves, vanilla beans, cumin and parsley.

Once, an entire shelf has been devoted to cookbooks boasting such delicacies as centipede fricassee, squirrel pie, snipe a l'orange, robin shish kebab, and, alas! rabbit au vin. The truth was that Mangle couldn't read at all, not even a recipe, but he'd liked having the cookbooks in the kitchen nevertheless. One day, however, the Baroness had discovered one of her own tomes entitled POISONED APPLES AND OTHER GIFTS FOR RIVALS among Mangle's cookbooks. Naturally, she had been rather upset. So all the books had to go. Now that shelf was used to hold a few pots of wilted scallions and a green tomato plant.

It was here in the kitchen that Mangle spent most of his time, polishing the silver or sharpening his kitchen knives and cleavers which he liked to keep razor sharp. The giant was occupied in this latter task and keeping his eye on a bubbling cauldron over the fire when Wallace awoke from the swoon he'd fallen into when Mangle had carried him off in the pocket of Herman's jacket. Wallace had remained unconscious for a long time, probably because the kitchen was so warm and because the terrors of the past two days had been so stressful. At any rate, when Wallace did awaken it was to a strange sound.

Zzzzzzzzst. Zzzzzzzzst. Zzzzzzzzst. Zzzzzzzzst.

Where am I? the mouse wondered groggily. In a horrible flash of memory he remembered the events of the past few hours and nearly swooned again. But what was that sound?

Zzzzzzzzst. Zzzzzzzzst. Zzzzzzzzst. Zzzzzzzzst.

Cautiously, the mouse peeked out under the pocket flap of the jacket which was lying on a table. There was Mangle at the other side of the kitchen sitting astride a grindstone, engrossed in sharpening a meat cleaver.

Zzzzzzzzst. Zzzzzzzzst. Zzzzzzzzst. Zzzzzzzzst.

The cleaver gleamed in the light from the open fire.

Zzzzzzzzst. Zzzzzzzzst. Zzzzzzzzst. Zzzzzzzzst.

The edge of the cleaver flashed and sparkled.

Zzzzzzzzst. Zzzzzzzzst. Zzzzzzzzst. Zzzzzzzzst.

The giant began to hum along with the grating and whirring of the grindstone. After a few introductory bars in an appropriate minor key, Mangle began to sing loudly to himself as he worked.

> "Sharpen your blade
> My Baroness bade.
> Grind your cleaver
> Tonight I'll eat liver.
> The fur we'll save
> Only meat I crave.
>
> So sharpen your razor,
> Add spices for flavor.
> Remove the bones neatly
> Leave in the fat completely.
> Strop, then chop.
> Strop, then chop."

Zzzzzzzzst. Zzzzzzzzst. Zzzzzzzzst. Zzzzzzzzst.

It was the most ghastly song Wallace had ever heard. He wasn't sure that he could bear to hear another verse. Would it be possible, he wondered, to drop to the floor and slip out of door before Mangle might turn from his work and spy him? Before the mouse could make up his mind what to do, Mangle's song ended and the giant rose from the grindstone and picked up Herman's jacket.

Wallace cowered deep in the pocket. Thick, blunt fingers probed through the jacket cloth. *The giant was going through Herman's jacket pockets!*

Now a huge finger slipped into the pocket that concealed Wallace. The jagged fingernail stabbed nearer . . . and nearer . . .

Wallace leaped!

But even with a head start the mouse didn't have a chance. In the next instant he felt himself lifted high in the air by his tail. He hung there helplessly

"It's the cauldron for you!" In two strides the giant had crossed the room and was dangling Wallace over the pot on the open fire.

Wallace looked down into the churning water. Bubbles of scalding steam rose upward to meet him. With a mighty effort, Wallace swung himself upward and sank his teeth into the giant's thumb.

"Yow!" Mangle screamed in pain and flung the mouse away from him.

Shaken but unhurt, Wallace bolted for the door but the giant was right behind him.

CLANG! The giant's iron boot came crashing down on the stone floor just missing Wallace's tail.

CLANG! The giant's boot whistled over Wallace's head. "Nearly got you!" he thundered as he tried again to stomp the panicked mouse.

CLANG! Sparks flew up as iron shocked upon stone, singeing Wallace's whiskers.

In spite of his terror Wallace could now see clearly that Mangle stood between him and the only apparent refuge—a mouse hole! Wallace had no choice. A bare second before Mangle could swing the great iron boot again, the frantic mouse slid between the giant's feet. With a desperate bound he reached the hole and slipped inside.

What he had mistaken for a mouse hole was actually a deep crack that went right through the wall. Beyond lay what appeared to be a labyrinth of cracks within the thick stone wall. Nonetheless, Wallace felt safe for the first time since he's arrived at the castle. Weak with relief, the mouse sat down to catch his breath and to decide on his next move.

Just as his little heart had almost begun to pump evenly again, a huge eye blinked at him through the crack. Mangle was watching him. Wallace's heart started to thump wildly again. Suddenly he was plunged into total darkness as the giant stuck his finger into the crack. Wallace drew back. The gigantic finger wiggled and probed but could not reach him.

"I'll have to get that good-for-nothing snake," said Mangle. "I can't reach in far enough. But the snake will be able to slip through." The finger withdrew.

This was all Wallace needed to hear. He stepped back into the dark passageway deep within the castle wall.

11

Herman awoke the next morning with a terrible sense of dread. That he had survived an evening and an entire night in the Baroness' castle should have given him renewed courage, but it didn't. What frightened him most was that he was all alone. Wallace had not returned all night.

When the giant had carried Wallace off in the pocket of his jacket, Herman had been heartsick with anxiety and a crushing sense of his own helplessness. He paced the floor of his bed chamber into the wee hours of the morning until he was utterly exhausted. Finally, he had lain back on the bed in his clothes, dozing fitfully.

Several times during the long night he awoke to loud clangs and thuds echoing through the castle. Once he thought he heard a steady scratching sound which seemed to be just outside the door of his bed chamber. He rushed to the door hoping it was Wallace. But when he opened the door, no one was there. The long corridor lay in total darkness.

Now somewhere in the castle a clock struck seven. The wizard's potion would wear off soon. What would he do then, he wondered. Oh, Wallace! Where are you? Cynthia-Seven, where are you?

He changed clothes, wanting to look composed and self-assured in case, heaven forbid, he ran into the Baroness. He had to use the mirror attached to the inside lid of his suitcase when he combed his hair as there was no mirror in his room. I suppose, he mused, this is another way to keep guests as uncomfortable as possible.

There was no one in the dim corridor when Herman stealthily opened the door and peeked out. He was nearly all the way down the stairs when he encountered the Baroness.

"Good morning!" Herman said much too loudly but as brightly as he could manage. He bowed low, hoping to brazen it out.

"Where are *you* going?"

"I . . . um . . . was looking you, dear lady."

"Why?"

"Uh . . ."

"Well?"

"Um . . . to bid you a good morning."

"What's good about it? There's a mouse loose in the castle."

"Nevertheless, how fine you look this morning, Baroness. Now I know what is meant by beauty sleep," Herman said, regaining his composure and attempting to distract the witch by appealing to her vanity.

"Oh," cooed the witch, momentarily soothed. "'Beauty sleep' did you say?"

"Well, that must be the reason you look so exceptional this morning. You must have slept comfortably."

At the idea of comfort, the Baroness bridled. "On the contrary, I had an awful night. The thought of a mouse loose in the castle kept me wide awake the entire night. But I will be quite myself at lunch later."

"Lunch? Later? Oh! Well, you see, Baroness, I am still a little weary from my journey so I suppose you won't mind if I skip lunch."

"I have to assume that you must not have gotten good grades in school for supposing."

"Oh," said Herman a little taken back. "Yet someone as important as yourself must have many pressing matters to attend to. So believe me, Baroness, when I say that I will understand completely if you might not be able to join me at lunch."

"You would miss me a little thought," asked the cunning Baroness.

"Oh, you needn't concern yourself about *me*."

"But you would be all alone?"

"I don't mind being alone. Not at all, I assure you, Baroness." He attempted to smile at the witch, feeling a little relieved.

"Of course, you won't be entirely alone. Mangle would be there serving." The witch chuckled, the sound like chalk scraping across a slate board.

"Oh . . . Mangle."

"But, even with Mangle there, would you still be lonely without *me*?" the witch asked, pressing her advantage.

"Ah . . . yes," Herman replied now rather wary.

"Don't mumble. Speak up."

"Yes, I would be lonely without your presence."

"Glad to hear you admit it. Since that is the case, I will reorganize my schedule so that I *can* join you for lunch—after all," the witch concluded triumphantly, bestowing on Herman her most horrific smile.

Before Herman could think of a rejoinder, Mangle appeared. He held up his bandaged thumb. "Vicious mouse . . . loose somewhere," the giant stammered. "I was bitten . . . on my thumb."

"I have already told Herman about the mouse. Come with me," she said to Mangle. "We'll get the snake to take care of that mouse." She turned to Herman. "I would advise you to practice your skills for I will expect you to demonstrate your magical powers at lunch this afternoon. Until then stay in your room. Don't wander around the castle." With that the witch rushed off leaving Herman with a sick feeling in the pit of his stomach.

Yet, the news that Wallace had not yet been captured gave him hope. He waited a few minutes and then made his way to the central foyer. Scores of passageways confronted him. Having nothing else to guide him, he picked one at random. At the end of this corridor there was a door. He tried it. The handle would not turn. It was locked. He retraced his steps to the central foyer and tried another door. This time the knob turned easily but with a rusty squeak. He held his breath. Had anyone heard? No one appeared. Gingerly, Herman opened the door. Behind it lay another long passageway. He followed it—right into the kitchen!

What luck! There was his jacket. He searched all the pockets. Empty! "Wallace!" he called. There was no answer.

Herman looked all about the room. Wallace was nowhere to seen. But, he thought, his spirits soaring at the possibility, Wallace may be hiding somewhere nearby.

With a final glance around to make sure he had not missed any clue as to the whereabouts of his friend, Herman retraced his steps down the hall. But somehow he must have made a wrong turn as he now found himself in front of a staircase leading downward. He debated for a moment whether or not to descend into the darkness below. Yet, if there was the slightest chance that this staircase might lead to Wallace or Cynthia-Seven, he felt he had to take it.

A blast of icy, stagnant air rose to meet him as he descended. Carefully, he felt his way downward. The stone walls were damp and clammy to the touch. Something spongy and slippery—moss or mold, he decided—grew on the walls and even on the stone steps themselves making his descent dangerous. He had to grasp the edges of the uneven stones of the wall to keep from slipping.

Finally, he reached the bottom. He now stood on the damp stone floor of the cellar beneath the castle. His eyes soon adjusted to the dimness and eventually he was able to make out dark outlines and vague shapes around him.

"Why this is a dungeon," he exclaimed aloud when he was able to make out a long row of cells. He tried each cell door as he made his way down the corridor. All of them were locked. He called softly at each door: "Wallace? Cynthia-Seven?"

No one answered.

At the end of that corridor he entered another long passageway. Here there was virtually no light at all. He felt his way along the wall when suddenly his skin turned to gooseflesh and the back of his neck prickled.

Someone or something was here in the darkness with him!

He stopped dead in his tracks. Should he go on or go back the way he had come? He listened. There was no sound. Perhaps it is just my nerves playing tricks on me, he told himself. I am pretty jittery.

He kept on walking and suddenly found himself staring down into two glowing purple eyes turned full upon him!

The snake, Herman thought in horror.

"Help," he shouted as the purple specter came toward him.

12

Wallace had spent a drafty, sleepless night in the deep recesses within the walls of the castle. The stones were icy and damp and now Wallace's cold was worse.

"Kerchoo! Kerchoo!" he sneezed hoping he would not be heard as the sound echoed deafeningly within the walls.

He was hopelessly lost in the maze of crevices and cracks within the walls. He had several bad moments when he thought about the possibility of coming face to face with the snake in this dark labyrinth within the castle walls.

I might die here, he worried. No one would ever find me—not even my skeleton. The mouse began to sob but the sound reverberated so loudly within those close quarters that he had to control himself or be deafened.

At the next turning he saw a dim light ahead. He went toward the light eagerly. It proved to be an opening in the wall! He was ecstatic and out he sprang into what at first he thought was a garden outside the castle. Everywhere he looked there were green plants and bushes.

An indoor greenhouse he soon realized. The vaulted ceiling was of frosted glass through which the winter sun poured with unusual strength. Rows and rows of potted plants and shrubs grew in wild abandon. It's like a jungle, Wallace thought, a bright, cheerful and *warm* jungle.

The variety was amazing. Small bonsai with turquoise fruit stood alongside lemony and cherry-hued trees. Plants of all kinds, neatly potted, stretched out in long rows. Their leaves were gorgeous but of the most unnatural colors: salmon, poppy, vivid scarlet, silver, violet, gentian, vermillion, indigo, cerise, henna, even jet black. Beyond, Wallace could see a series of smaller rooms branching off this one. The first he entered contained groups of exotic flowering plants decorated with a black ribbon.

How odd, Wallace mused in amazement. He was about to bend over to smell a particularly lovely ruby and fuchsia cluster of petals when he noticed a sign hanging above him: POISONS.

What a close call, he realized. Yet, everything is so beautiful. How could such beauty be poisonous he wondered. But the more Wallace stared, the more menacing the plants seemed until he began to imagine that he could see the terrible poisons drip off those beautiful petals. He backed out of the room carefully to avoid the slightest contact with any of these poisonous flowers and entered the last hot house.

Here basket upon basket of common garden vegetables crowded the room. Purple beets, white turnips, yellow squash, red cabbages, orange carrots, golden wax beans, peas in their bright green pods.

This must be the Baroness' vegetable garden he reckoned. Imagine having fresh vegetables in the middle of winter! An irresistible urge came over the mouse for he adored green peas and he was very hungry as it had had no dinner. He popped a handful of peas into his mouth and swallowed them practically whole. Delicious! He reached for another handful. Too late he noticed the sign hung above: POTIONS—POWERFUL.

Wallace gasped and dropped the peas he was holding in his hand. What have I done?

Almost immediately the mouse turned a bright tangerine. A second later that brilliant hue faded to rosy pick, fading in its turn to powder blue and finally brightening again to purple—even his eyes. Wallace remained purple but he didn't know it.

I guess I'm must be all right, thought the mouse with relief when he felt no change in himself. I'll bet the Baroness just put that sign up to keep anyone else from eating her vegetables. Then he chanced to look down at his feet.

"What's happened to my feet! They're purple!" he howled. He held up his paws. They were purple too. "*I'm* purple" he screeched as the truth penetrated.

The mouse dashed to and fro, wailing: "Oh, oh, oh!" His eyes were filled with tears so he didn't see the open trap door until he fell through it.

13

It was the most awful moment of Herman's young life when he came face to face with the purple specter. It was probably the happiest moment of his life when he recognized the purple-eyed specter. It was Wallace but a very wretched Wallace indeed.

"Wallace!" Herman gasped, still not fully recovered from his fright. "Is it really you?"

"Oh, Herman!" cried the mouse, overcome and bursting into tears of relief. "Id's me. I'm so happy I found you. I thought I'd never see you again."

"I thought the same thing. But what's happened to you?"

"Just look at me!" The mouse sobbed piteously.

"You are rather purple," admitted Herman tenderly, "if you don't mind my saying so. But you seem to be you . . . er . . . otherwise. And it is a nice color, a bright purple."

"Bedda than gray?"

Herman sidestepped the question. "How did you get this way?"

So Wallace choked out the story of his escape from Mangle in the kitchen and his lonely night in the cracks within the castle walls.

"Peas?" Herman reiterated as Wallace concluded his tale of woe. Herman wasn't sure that he'd heard correctly. "Peas? Why in the world did you eat them?"

"That's fine for *you* to ask," snapped the mouse. "After stuffing yourself at the Baroness' table. I was there. I saw you. Well, in case you're interested, I missed *my* supper."

"As long as you feel all right, Wallace, perhaps it won't really matter—being purple and all. It is an awfully nice color, very bright and cheerful. One of my favorites. Really it is," Herman offered in a soothing voice

"Oh, yeah? How would you like to be purple?"

"Well, *I* certainly would never have been foolish enough to have eaten those peas."

"Is that so?" spat out Wallace in a fury. "You haven't had to go through what I've had to go through. I heard you all during dinner, enjoying yourself, having a high old time, flirting with that ugly Baroness, praising thad snake—"

"—Now that's not fair, Wallace. We've both had our trials and—"

"—Have I gotten any sympathy at all? Or, have I gotten any credit for my daring escape from Mangle? I bid him on the thumb, you know."

"Well, of course, you were very brave," Herman began, frowning. "We both have been brave for that matter and—"

"—And why didn't you DO something when Mangle dragged me off?"

"I couldn't do anything, Wallace. I wanted to, of course. But there was nothing I could do. Nothing at all."

"You could at the very least have looked for me, couldn't you?" Wallace was practically screaming.

"You are being unfair," Herman said as calmly as he was able. "I waited for you to come back to the room. I couldn't stumble around in the dark during the night. I had to wait until morning to search for you."

"Unfair? Unfair?"

"I've been the one on the firing line, Wallace. Not you. I've had to do everything—all the thinking, all the planning, all the fast talking. What have you done except to complicate matters and make the witch suspicious and—"

"—Complicate matters! So thad's how you really feel." The mouse's voice rose an octave. "So that's the thanks I ged. All right. All right. I should have known bedda. I guess you would have been happier if you never saw me again." The mouse turned on his heel and started walking away. Though quite slowly.

"Wait, Wallace. That's not true. I am overjoyed to see you again. I was very, very worried about you. I'm so glad we are reunited again. Don't be angry. Have you forgotten what brought us here to the Baroness' castle?"

Wallace hung his head. "You're right, Herman."

"I'm sorry for what I said to upset you. We are both under a great deal of stress. Have you seen any sign of Cynthia-Seven?"

"Nod a trace. How about you?"

Downcast, Herman shook his head sadly. "Not a trace."

14

The long dim corridor leading back to Herman's bed chamber seemed to stretch out for miles before them. They were both dejected and beginning to feel so hopeless that they probably never would have seen the metal ring almost flush with the wall if Wallace hadn't brushed against it.

"What's this?"

"Where?"

"Here in the wall. A ring."

"It's a handle," observed Herman. "Look closely. There's a concealed door here."

Except for a nearly imperceptible crack running around its rim, the door was virtually invisible to any eye but an informed one.

"Should we?"

"Led's."

Exerting all his might, Herman pulled on the metal ring. With a dreadful creak the huge door swung open easily. Beyond lay a narrow stone staircase leading upward.

"The tower," they said in unison.

They mounted the steps. Herman let the door close behind them. But as the door eased into place nearly all of the light was cut off.

"It's too dark in here," murmured Wallace.

"Stay close."

They climbed slowly. The steps and the walls, like those in the cellar below, were damp and icy to the touch.

"All these freezing places are certainly not helping me get rid of my cold," Wallace complained. "I've already lost my sense of smell completely."

The steps seemed endless. "99, 100, 101, 102," Herman counted aloud as this helped him to feel less afraid in the darkness. On the count of 103 Herman struck his head on the ceiling!

"What's the matter?" asked Wallace just before he passed Herman and hit his head against the ceiling also.

"This is impossible. A staircase doesn't lead to a ceiling. Herman rubbed his head. "Is this is a trap door?"

It was a trap door. Shoulders together (Wallace stood on the highest step, level with Herman's nose), they pushed. Peering through the opening, they saw the turret chamber, stacked high on all sides with cages piled upon cages. A small barred window admitted the only light.

Something moved in one of the cages far across the chamber, something large and black.

"CYNTHIA-SEVEN!"

In the next instant they were bounding joyfully across the room. It was Cynthia-Seven but she had changed considerable since Herman and Wallace had seen her last. She was enormous! Rolls upon rolls of fat encircled her body. Her lovely blue eyes looked out at them from a huge, round ball of fur. Even her ears seemed larger.

"Oh, Cynthia-Seven! We came to the witch's castle to save you but we thought we'd never see you again."

"Wallace?" she screeched. "Wallace, is *that* you?" The rabbit tried to reach out to him through the bars of her cage but her paw was too fat. "What's happened to you. You're all purple!"

"Never mind about that," snapped Wallace. "It's me just the same but I'd rather not discuss it except to say that I feel perfectly all right except for my cold." In a kinder tone, he asked: "Are you all right, dear?"

"I am so glad to see you both. How incredibly brave of you to come to the witch's castle to rescue me." She began to cry. "I've been so lonely and frightened," she whimpered.

"It must have been awful for you."

Cynthia-Seven sobbed even harder.

"Don't cry, dear. We'll get you out of here," said Herman.

"You look . . . er . . . fine," offered Wallace, hoping to console her.

"Do I? I suppose that I've put on a little weight. I can't help it. The meals are really so delicious!" She sighed. "Mangle comes up to feed me everyday, about this time."

Wallace glanced nervously around.

"He brings trays of such fattening foods. I have nothing else to do all day, so I eat."

"Don't you know why you're being fed so much?"

The rabbit hung her head and two huge tears escaped from beneath the lowered lashes. "I can't help it."

"Well, you bedda."

"Never mind that now. We're going to get you out right now." Herman flipped the latch and the cage door swung open.

"Come on. Hurry."

"Oh," exclaimed the rabbit as she tried to slip out of the cage. She was too fat. "Help me."

Wallace was about to get into the cage to push while Herman was about to pull when they all heard a loud CLANG! The door at the foot of the stairs had been opened!

Clump! CLUMP! Clump! CLUMP! Clump! CLUMP!

"Mangle's coming!"

"Hide!"

Herman slammed the cage door shut. With one bound he and Wallace dove behind a pile of cages. Just in time, for at that moment the trap door flew open and Mangle's gigantic head appeared in the opening.

"Hello, my pretty," he boomed. "Here's your dinner." The giant bore a large tray loaded with aromatic dishes. Strawberries drowning in rich thick cream. Candied baby carrots in sweet honey syrup. Crisp lettuce and other garden greens bathed in mayonnaise. Steaming cabbage soup, chunky and creamy.

Mangle opened the cage door. Cynthia-Seven screamed as he prodded her in the ribs.

"Ha, ha, ha," he chuckled. "You're getting nice and fat. Just a few more pounds. So eat hearty."

Without so much as a glance around, Mangle closed the cage and headed back down the stairs. "Eat hearty," he said again as he lowered the trap door over his head. "I'll be back with dessert."

"Don't eat any of thad!"

But Cynthia-Seven had already popped a strawberry into her mouth.

"Stop this instant!"

"I know, but one strawberry can't make a difference," she said as she cleverly palmed a second strawberry. "I won't touch another morsel."

"You bedda not," warned Wallace.

"We have to go because Mangle might be on his way back."

"You're not going leave me here, are you?" moaned the rabbit in dismay.

"We must. We can't take you with us now because Mangle will be coming back and he will see that you're missing. Also I have to get my suitcase. We'll come back for you when the coast is clear."

"Oh, dear, oh, dear," she whimpered. "Do you have a plan?"

"Not yet, but I'm working on one," answered Herman. "Don't worry. We'll come back for you very soon."

"Led's hurry! And don't eat any more of that food," Wallace hissed.

"If only I go could with you . . . NOW."

"It's not possible. We'll come back. We promise."

"Remember, don't eat any more of that food."

"We'll be back . . ."

They were heading down the corridor toward Herman's room when they saw Mangle coming up the stairs. There was just enough time for Wallace to scurry around the corner. Mangle never noticed the fleeting purple streak.

"The Baroness Meen wishes to speak to you," he announced. "Follow me."

"Now?"

"NOW!"

Herman felt he couldn't refuse to accompany the giant although he was extremely worried about Wallace who would be waiting in the drafty corridor until he returned. With the snake on the loose, it was not a safe place for the mouse. Reluctantly, he followed Mangle down the stairs, glancing ruefully back over his shoulder.

Wallace, on the other hand, never looked back. He felt awful. His cold was worse and he couldn't breathe through his nose at all. Most of all though he hated being purple. But that they had actually located Cynthia-Seven and that she was really none the worse for the experience was worth everything!

The mouse paced up and down the drafty corridor for a while. But then, hoping to find a warmer spot to wait for Herman, he followed the corridor to the end where it turned to the left. Had Wallace not had a cold and had he not lost his sense of smell, he would *never* have turned down that corridor because the aroma of almonds would certainly have warned him.

15

A library!" exclaimed Wallace with pleasure as he peeked through an open door at the end of the corridor. It was an impressive room lined on three sides from floor to ceiling with shelves of musty leather-bound books.

This must be the witch's private collection, the mouse decided. Perhaps there will be something here to help me to get back to my own natural color.

The lower shelves, those that Wallace could see most easily, contained ghost stories and murder mysteries. A group of worn leather bound volumes high up on a shelf near the ceiling caught his eye.

He shinnied up the wall, using the jutting shelves as a staircase. The titles were faded but still quite legible. SPELLS FOR SPITE was the first. I know I'm on the right track now, Wallace thought. PRESTO POTIONS was the next tome. He read on: SLIGHT OF HAND NOW QUICK AND EASY . . . VOO DOO YOU DO . . . ILLUSIONS FOR FUN AND PROFIT . . . EVERYMAN'S

BOOK OF CURSES . . . GRANDMUMMY'S OLD FASHIONED MAGIC. The next, a slim volume, was entitled POTIONS AND THEIR UNDOING. Just the thing!

Wallace tugged at it. It slid easily out of the tightly packed shelf and then, as if it had a life of its own, it fell off the shelf, landing on a chair below.

Wallace scampered down after it. On the far wall the curtains around the windows were drawn back so there was a good light for reading. Wallace had just climbed up into the chair where the book had so conveniently landed when all at once the fur on the back of his head stood up straight.

Did a curtain move? The mouse looked around the room. Nonsense. I'm getting too jumpy, he chided himself.

He settled back comfortably against the soft cushions, his back to the light from the windows. He opened the book and began to leaf slowly through the pages.

What was that? He saw the curtains rippling slightly in the wind that leaked around the window frame. He turned back to his book and soon was checking the index: abracadabra . . .. . . afoul . . . oh, my how sad he thought and felt his own tail to make sure it was still there. He continued . . . agony . . . alarm . . . ammonia . . . antidote! Here it is! He bent lower over the book, totally engrossed.

A small black head eased itself from under the folds of the window curtains and looked around.

Wallace felt uneasy. He couldn't shake the feeling that someone was watching him. Perhaps I am running a temperature, he thought, and resumed reading.

The snake's long thin body oozed slowly forward like flowing water.

The mouse squirmed uncomfortably in his chair. My nerves are shot and I am way too jittery, he told himself.

The snake slithered closer to Wallace's chair.

Wallace turned a page in the book.

The snake gained another yard.

I can't seem to concentrate, the mouse thought, and shut the book with a loud clap. Immediately the snake popped back under the curtains. Wallace looked around nervously but seeing nothing settled deeper into the cushions of the chair.

The black head reappeared from behind the curtains. Slowly, it inched toward Wallace, its beady purple eyes riveted on the mouse.

Wallace opened the book again and began to read.

The snake reached the rug where it was perfectly camouflaged against its thick black wavy-lined design.

Wallace suddenly felt warm. I know I have a fever, he thought.

The snake edged nearer. The floor creaked. Wallace started so violently that he nearly fell out of the chair. The snake lay perfectly still. Wallace leaned over and looked around the side of his chair but the snake's coils were indiscernible against the black wavy lines of the patterned rug.

Dear me! I wish I could calm down, he thought as he sank back uneasily into the cushions again. My nerves are really in terrible shape.

The black head lifted up from the design in the carpet. The snake slithered closer to Wallace's chair. And closer yet.

Wallace turned another page in the book.

The snake reached the back of Wallace's chair. Its body became a stiff rope. Up rose the head. It swayed just above the high back of the chair. Its eyes bore into the back of Wallace's neck.

The mouse's nose itched annoyingly but he kept on reading.

The shinny black head hovered over him. Its forked tongue flickered in and out of the narrow slit in its jaw as the snake savored the prospect before him.

Wallace read on.

Just then the library door was pushed wide open. "Here you are!" shouted Herman from the doorway. "I've been looking—WALLACE! *The snake! Behind you!*" he screamed just as the snake struck.

Wallace, already jumpy, needed no second notice. He leaped straight into the air, every purple hair on his body standing on end. Out of the corner of his eye he saw the terrible black head whiz by his shoulder. *The snake missed him!* In that moment of supreme terror Wallace's hair turned back to its natural gray!

Without touching the floor, the mouse rotated in mid-air and attained the doorway in a single bound. Herman slammed the library door after them. Down the corridor they raced and did not stop for a breath until they reached Herman's bed chamber.

Wallace, understandably, was a wreck. He shook and gasped, repeating over and over: "Just think! It was in the room with me all the time." He paced up and down the floor. "In the room with me all thad time. All thad time."

"Try to relax, Wallace," Herman said as gently as possible. "At least you are your old self again." He held his suitcase open so the mouse would view his reflection in the mirror glued to the inside of the lid.

"It wasn't worth it," responded the mouse, smoothing down his coat where the fur in places still stood on end. "Although I do look good in spite of everything."

"You do but I have to tell you the latest. The Baroness is suspicious of me. Mangle reported that he heard my voice in the cellar. She demanded to know why I was roaming around in the castle when she'd told me to stay in my room. She presented me with an ultimatum. I am to meet with her in an hour to prove that I am her equal in magic. If I can't, I am to be thrown off the cliff."

Wallace was so horrified he couldn't speak for a moment. Finally he managed: "Whad about me?"

"If you're found, you're to be fed to the snake."

The news was too much for the mouse. Wallace fainted.

16

When Wallace regained consciousness a few moments later, Herman was bending over him, anxiously.

"What will we do?" mumbled the mouse weakly.

"We must get Cynthia-Seven immediately. Then we'll just have to make a run for it."

"A run for it—now? Shouldn't we wait for dark?"

"We can't delay any longer. Zachery Tack's potion has probably worn off. Every moment we wait the danger increases." Herman, his features set with determination, picked up his suitcase. "Let's go. Now!"

The pair flew up the stone staircase to the tower and soon stood in front of Cynthia-Seven's cage.

"Wallace, you're your old self again. How wonderful."

"We're getting you out of there right now."

Herman lifted the latch. The cage door swung open but, of course, Cynthia-Seven didn't come bounding out.

Wallace slipped into the back of the cage. The rabbit strained to squeeze out of the door. Herman pulled with all his might. Wallace pushed from the rear.

"Eck! Ow! I can't," she cried.

"Push," said Herman but Cynthia-Seven couldn't be budged.

"Oh, woe is me, I'll be here *forever*," she wailed.

"'Forever?' No, you won't. If we don't get you out of there now, Mangle will get you out one day."

That thought gave the rabbit renewed will.

"Push harder, Wallace."

"Ow!"

"Once more. Everybody. On the count of three."

"OUCH!" A few clumps of black fur clung to the edge of the cage door but Cynthia-Seven was free.

There was no one in the corridor and, thankfully, no one appeared when the metal ring on the hidden tower door slipped from Herman's grasp and the door closed with a resounding *bang*! They tore down the long staircase to the main foyer. Where was the front door? They faced scores of arches and doors all of which looked exactly alike.

"There!" cried Wallace, pointing.

"Run," shouted Herman, needlessly.

They were only yards from the front door when a dreadful but familiar voice rang out: "STOP!"

They turned. There stood the Baroness Meen, Mangle at her side brandishing his gleaming cleaver.

"Do something!" Cynthia-Seven squealed.

"You keep strange company I see. What's the meaning of this?"

"We're leaving—all three of us. Right now."

"We'll see about that," the witch announced ripping the black patch from her eye.

"Quick. Get behind me." Herman flung himself down on the floor and in the same motion threw up the lid of his suitcase like a shield in front of them.

A white flash leaped across the foyer in waves of near-blinding light. It hit the suitcase with a crash like a great explosion and ricocheted off, swooping and bouncing like a bolt of lightning gone berserk.

"Look out! Look out!"

The flash continued to bounce wildly. Not *at* the trio crouched behind the upraised lid of Herman's suitcase, but *away* from them!

Mangle saw it coming and but he was too huge to move quickly, and the cold white light swept over him and the witch.

The air turned frigid. A powdery frost formed on everything. Instantly, the Baroness and Mangle were turned into statues of ice, Mangle still in the act of raising his cleaver.

"How dreadful! Even for them," said Cynthia-Seven when she realized that both the witch and the giant were frozen solid.

"How did you do thad?" Wallace asked with trepidation.

"Don't worry. Not with magic."

"Nod with magic. Are you sure?"

"None at all," Herman assured him. "Since we arrived I've been puzzled about why there aren't any mirrors in the castle."

"Mirrors?"

"Yes. Mirrors. I don't suppose that you've noticed but there isn't a single mirror anywhere in the castle. After a while it hit me! The Baroness must be afraid of mirrors."

"Afraid? Of mirrors? Why?"

"Exactly what I asked myself. Why? And now you can see why for yourself," said Herman gesturing toward the gruesome statues. "A mirror reflects what is put in front of it. The Baroness could never take the chance of coming upon one unawares for a mirror would reflect her own gaze back upon her."

"So that's why you had us get behind your suitcase — because of the mirror on the inside lid."

"Exactly."

"So the Baroness looked directly into your mirror and her gaze was turned back on herself and Mangle."

"Exactly."

"You are marvelously clever, Herman," bubbled Cynthia-Seven. "To think that you were able to outwit the witch without any magic at all. Just by your own wits!" The rabbit glanced at Wallace who seemed to be pouting. "Of course, I know how brave and helpful you have been too, Wallace. I think you are both wonderful."

"I guess I have always had a healthy respect for using my brains," admitted Herman, his old self-assurance reasserting itself again.

"The witch will never harm anyone else ever again," said Wallace.

"Nor will Mangle ever hunt in our forest again," added Cynthia-Seven, casting a last glance at the grotesque figure of ice.

Nonetheless, the trio bolted out the front door and in a moment they were breathing the first fresh, untroubled air they had inhaled in days.

In the daylight the trip back to the forest was almost pleasant, their only anxious moment when they reached the river. It was frozen solid again so they had no difficulty crossing over though Wallace never took his eyes off the ice as he raced over it.

Cynthia-Seven was overjoyed to see her burrow again. Herman, with Wallace's invaluable help, wrote out a strict diet for Cynthia-Seven and spent the next few weeks checking to make sure she kept on it. Of course, she never became a really slender rabbit but they never had the heart to tell her.

Herman never went back to the orphanage. Instead, he went to live with Zachery Tack who built a small boat so they could cross the river to visit their friends in the forest whenever they wished. The cats got used to Wallace's visits but Wallace was never totally at ease when he and Cynthia-Seven visited Herman at the wizard's home.

Herman had hoped to study magic spells under Zachery Tack's tutelage but the wizard was so forgetful that he could never remember the right words or the correct ingredients. So Herman was forced to study magic from a book. The only book on magic he could find in the public library was one on prestidigitation and illusion.

Of course, this wasn't real magic. In fact, when Herman thought things over, he was fairly sure that nothing that had happened during his adventure had anything to do with magic. There was an explanation for everything.

The tricks he was able to do always involved clever deceptions to gain their effect. He practiced faithfully and finally got good enough to go on tour. He invited

Cynthia-Seven to go along as part of his act, though she was certainly a hefty rabbit to pull out of a hat.

At first Wallace didn't want to be reminded of anything that had to do with magic, even Herman's pretend kind, but, of course, he didn't want to be separated from his friends. So in the end he agreed to go on tour. He claimed the title of "Prop Manager" and wore a red hat with his name and title embroidered on the brim. And not long after he heard the thunderous applause that Herman and Cynthia-Seven received after each performance, he began to study Herman's book of card tricks late at night when everyone was asleep.

The End